Tug of War

John Burningham

RED FOX

For my mother, who introduced me to African folk tales

TUG OF WAR
A RED FOX BOOK 978 1 849 41807 2

First published in Great Britain by Jonathan Cape,
an imprint of Random House Children's Publishers UK
A Random House Group Company

Jonathan Cape edition published 2012
Red Fox edition published 2013

1 3 5 7 9 10 8 6 4 2

Illustrations copyright © John Burningham, 1968
Text copyright © John Burningham, 2012

Red Fox Books are published by Random House Children's Publishers UK,
61–63 Uxbridge Road, London W5 5SA

www.**randomhousechildrens**.co.uk
www.**randomhouse**.co.uk

Addresses for companies within The Random House Group Limited can be found at: www.randomhouse.co.uk/offices.htm

THE RANDOM HOUSE GROUP Limited Reg. No. 954009

A CIP catalogue record for this book is available from the British Library.

Printed in China

The Random House Group Limited supports the Forest Stewardship Council® (FSC®),
the leading international forest certification organization. Our books carrying the FSC label are printed on
FSC®-certified paper. FSC is the only forest certification scheme endorsed by the leading environmental organizations,
including Greenpeace. Our paper procurement policy can be found at www.randomhouse.co.uk/environment.

Hare, Hippopotamus and Elephant lived in the forest, as they
had done for thousands and thousands of years. But often, when
Hippopotamus and Elephant had nothing better to do, they would
be horrid to Hare and tease him.

Hippopotamus would say to Hare,
"What a tiny, weedy thing you are
with those ridiculous long ears.
All you can do is hop about."

And Elephant would say, "Hare, you really are a feeble idiot with your twitching nose and those whiskers. That's all you have."

Now Hare was getting very fed up with Hippopotamus and Elephant being nasty to him day after day, so he thought of a plan. Hare went first to see Elephant.

"Elephant," said Hare, "if we were to have a tug of war together, I think I would win."

"You must be joking, you sickly little twit," said Elephant. "I am two hundred million times stronger than you." Nevertheless, Hare gave Elephant one end of the rope and then went down to the river to speak to Hippopotamus.

"What on earth do you want now, you silly long-eared, big-whiskered NURD," said Hippopotamus.

"Although you think I am tiny and weedy, if you could find the time to have a tug of war with me," said Hare, "I know I would win."

"You! Win against me? You must be joking!" said Hippopotamus. "There is no way a twitty little twink like you could possibly win against mighty me."

"Go on then, off you go into the trees,"
said Hippopotamus, taking the other end
of the rope. "When you start to pull, I'll tug
so hard you'll be flicked into the river."

Hare stood inbetween Elephant
and Hippotamus and tugged the rope.
Hippotamus in the river felt the tug
and started to pull.

Elephant in the forest felt the tug and was amazed
at what he thought was the strength of Hare.

And the tug of war began. Elephant
and Hippopotamus could not believe
how hard Hare was pulling the rope.

They pulled at twilight.
They pulled at sunset.

And they pulled all through the night.

Hare went as close as he could to Hippopotamus without being seen. "Oh, Hippopotamus, are you not tired yet? You have been pulling for such a long time. Won't you say I am as good as you?" "No, I won't, you sickly little twit," said Hippopotamus, and pulled even harder.

Hare went close to Elephant and whispered,
"Have you had enough, Elephant? Will you say
I am the winner?"
"Not in a million years will you ever win against
me," said Elephant, and pulled with all his might.

Hippopotamus pulled hard but by now
he was getting very tired and could not
understand why Hare was not moving,
and how he could be so strong.

Hare went over to Elephant.

"Have you had enough, Elephant?

Do you admit I am better than you?"

"Oh, Hippopotamus," said Hare, going near to the river. "Surely you must now agree I am the stronger?"

After some time, Elephant and Hippopotamus finally stopped pulling and began slowly walking towards Hare at the other end of the rope. "What are you doing here, Hippotamus?" said Elephant. "I thought I was having a tug of war with Hare?"

"So did I," said Hippopotamus. They were both furious and realized they had been tricked. "Let's get the little runt!" they said and thundered off to find Hare.

"We'll search every inch of the forest until we find that weedy little twink and then we'll sort him out," they said.

But even though they charged about
for hours, they would never find Hare,
because he was already miles away
up in the hills.
For Hare had proved that although
he was not as strong as them, he
was perhaps a bit more clever.